Critical acclaim for Robert Crais

'Crais tells a compelling tale that glints with wit, intelligence and expertise'   *Literary Review*

'Far and away the most satisfying private eye novel in years'   *Lawrence Block*

'The kind of bravura performance only a pro can give'   *Kirkus Reviews*

'Terrific ... should be mentioned in the same breath as Robert B. Parker, Tony Hillerman, Sue Grafton and James Lee Bruke'   *Houston Chronicle*

'Crais is in a class by himself – he is quite simply the best'   *Eric Van Lustbarder*

'Crais knows his way around a wisecrack and a narrative sucker-punch ... enormously appealing'   *San Francisco Chronicle*

'Outstanding characters, tight plot and scintillating prose style'   *Mystery Scene Magazine*

'Intelligent, perceptive, hard, clean'   *James Ellroy*

'Crais is a terrific writer'   *Sue Grafton*

Robert Crais is the bestselling author of the Elvis Cole detective novels, winning awards and top-flight reviews. He lives in Los Angeles.

Demolition Angel

Robert Crais

ORION

An Orion paperback
First published in Great Britain by Orion in 2000
This paperback edition published in 2000 by

Orion Books Ltd,
Orion House, 5 Upper St Martin's Lane, London WC2H 9EA

A CIP catalogue record for this book
is available from the British Library.

ISBN O 75283 732 X

Typeset by Deltatype Ltd, Birkenhead, Merseyside
Printed and bound in Great Britain by
Clays Ltd, St Ives plc

For Jeffrey and Celia

ACKNOWLEDGMENTS

The author wishes to thank the following people for their help: Det. John Petievich, LAPD (retired); Det. Paul Bishop, LAPD; Det. Bob Nelson, Criminal Conspiracy Section, LAPD (retired); Lt Mike DeCoudres, commanding officer, LAPD Bomb Squad; Sgt Joe Pau, supervisor, LAPD Bomb Squad; Lt Anthony Alba, LAPD Public Affairs; Special Agent Charles Hustmyer, ATF; Stephen B. Scheid, Explosives Specialist, ATF; Marc Scott Taylor, Technical Associates, Inc.; Steven B. Richlin, OD; Jane Bryson, Ph.D.; Angela Donahue, Ph.D., Behavioral Science Unit, LAPD; Patricia Crais; Celia Gleason; Clay Fourrier; Leslie Day; Tami Hoag; Gerald Petievich; Shawn Coyne; Steve Rubin; Gina Centrello; Aaron Priest; Norman Kurland; Emile Gladstone; Tricia Davey; Jonathan King; and Laurence Mark.

The explosives experts and bomb technicians with whom I spoke were justifiably concerned that this book neither be instructional, nor reveal the exact capabilities by which bomb techs ply their trade. To that end, I have changed certain facts and procedures and fictionalized others. Professionals knowledgeable in the field should note that the technical and procedural inaccuracies contained in this work are the author's responsibility, and his alone.

PROLOGUE

To be disrupted: when the human body is
blown apart; as by the pressure force of a bomb.
– *Gradwohl's Legal Medicine*

Code Three Roll Out
Bomb Squad
Silver Lake, California

Charlie Riggio stared at the cardboard box sitting beside the Dumpster. It was a Jolly Green Giant box, with what appeared to be a crumpled brown paper bag sticking up through the top. The box was stamped GREEN BEANS. Neither Riggio nor the two uniformed officers with him approached closer than the corner of the strip mall there on Sunset Boulevard; they could see the box fine from where they were.

'How long has it been there?'

One of the Adam car officers, a Filipino named Ruiz, checked his watch.

'We got our dispatch about two hours ago. We been here since.'

'Find anyone who saw how it got there?'

'Oh, no, dude. Nobody.'

The other officer, a black guy named Mason, nodded.

'Ruiz is the one saw it. He went over and looked in the bag, the crazy Flip.'

'So tell me what you saw.'

'I told your sergeant.'

'Tell *me*. I'm the sonofabitch who's gonna approach the damned thing.'

Ruiz described seeing the capped ends of two galvanized pipes taped together with silver duct tape. The pipes were loosely wrapped in newspaper, Ruiz said, so he had only seen the ends.

Riggio considered that. They were standing in a strip mall on Sunset Boulevard in Silver Lake, an area that had

3

seen increasing gang activity in recent months. Gang-bangers would steal galvanized pipe from construction sites or dig up plastic PVC from some poor bastard's garden, then stuff them with bottle rocket powder or match heads. Riggio didn't know if the Green Giant box held an actual bomb or not, but he had to approach it as if it did. That's the way it was with bomb calls. Better than ninety-five percent turned out to be hairspray cans, some teenager's book bag, or, like his most recent call-out, two pounds of marijuana wrapped in Pampers. Only one out of a hundred was what the bomb techs called an 'improvised munition'.

A homemade bomb.

'You hear ticking or anything like that?'

'No.'

'Smell anything burning?'

'Uh-uh.'

'Did you open the bag to get a better look?'

'Hell, no.'

'Did you move the box or anything?'

Ruiz smiled like Riggio was nuts.

'Dude, I saw those pipes and shit my pants. The only thing I moved was my *feet*!'

Mason laughed.

Riggio walked back to his vehicle. The Bomb Squad drove dark blue Suburbans, rigged with a light bar and crammed with all the tools of the bomb technician's trade, except for the robots. You wanted the robots, you had to call them out special, and he wasn't going to do that. The goddamned robot would just get bogged down in all the potholes around the box.

Riggio found his supervisor, Buck Daggett, instructing a uniformed sergeant to evacuate the area for a hundred yards in all directions. The fire department had already been called, and paramedics were on the way. Sunset Boulevard had been closed and traffic rerouted. All for something that might turn out to be some do-it-yourself plumber's cast-off drain trap.

4

'Hey, Buck, I'm ready to take a look at that thing.'

'I want you in the suit.'

'It's too hot. I'll use the chest protector for the first pass, then the suit if I have to bring out the de-armer.'

All Riggio would be doing on the first pass was lugging out a portable X-ray to see inside the bag. If the contents appeared to be a bomb, he and Daggett would formulate a game plan and either de-arm the device or explode it in place.

'I want you in the suit, Charles. I got a feeling about this one.'

'You've always got a feeling.'

'I've also got the sergeant stripes. You're in the suit.'

The armored suit weighed almost ninety pounds. Made of Kevlar plates and heavy Nomex batting, it covered every part of Riggio's body except his hands, which remained bare. A bomb tech needed the dexterity of unencumbered fingers.

When the suit was in place, Riggio took the Real Time RTR3 X-ray unit and lumbered toward the package. Walking in the suit was like walking with his body wrapped in wet quilts, only hotter. Three minutes in the armor, and sweat was already running into his eyes. To make it worse, a safety cable and hardwire dragged behind him, the hardwire connecting him to Daggett via a Telex communicator. A separate wire linked the Real Time to a computer in the Suburban's cargo bay. He felt like he was pulling a plow.

Daggett's voice came into Riggio's ear. 'How you doing out there?'

'Sweating my ass off, thanks to you.'

Riggio hated this part the most, approaching an object before he knew what it was. Every time was the same: Riggio thought of that unknown object as a living beast with a life and a mind. Like a sleeping pit bull. If he approached it carefully and made the right moves, everything would be fine. If he startled the dog, the damn thing would rip him apart.

5

Eighty-two slow-motion paces brought him to the box. It was unremarkable except for a wet stain on one corner that looked like dog piss. The brown paper bag, crumpled and uneven, was open. Riggio peered into the bag without touching it. Leaning over was hard, and when he did, sweat dripped onto the Lexan faceplate like rain.

He saw the two pipes that Ruiz had described. The pipe caps appeared to be about two and a half inches in diameter and taped together, but nothing else about them was visible. They were loosely wrapped with newspaper, leaving only the ends exposed. Daggett said, 'How's it look?'

'Like a couple of pipes. Stand by. I'll get us a picture.'

Riggio placed the Real Time RTR3 on the ground at the base of the box, aimed for a side view, then turned on the unit. It provided the same type of translucent shadow image that security personnel see on airline baggage units, reproducing the image on two screens: one for Riggio on top of the RTR3 and another on the computer back at the Suburban.

Charlie Riggio smiled.

'Sonofabitch. We got one, Buck. We got us a bomb.'

'I'm seeing it.'

The two pipes were impenetrable shadows with what appeared to be a spool of wire or fuse triangled between them. There didn't appear to be a timer or an initiator of a more sophisticated nature, leading Riggio to believe that the bomb was a garage project made by an enterprising local gangbanger. Low-tech, dirty, and not particularly difficult to de-arm.

'This one's going to be a piece of cake, Buck. I make a basic fuse of the light-it-and-run-like-hell variety.'

'You be careful. Might be some kind of motion switch tucked away in there.'

'I'm not gonna touch it, Buck. Jesus. Gimme some credit.'

'Don't get cocky. Take the snaps and let's figure out what's what.'

The procedure was to take a series of digital computer snaps of the device via the Real Time at forty-five-degree angles. When they had the device mapped, Riggio would fall back to the Suburban, where he and Daggett would decide how best to destroy or de-arm it.

Riggio shuffled around the box, aiming the Real Time over the different angles. He felt no fear as he did this because he knew what he was dealing with now and trusted he could beat it. Riggio had approached over forty-eight suspicious packages in his six years with the Bomb Squad; only nine had been actual explosive devices. None of those had ever detonated in a manner that he did not control.

'You're not talking to me, Charlie. You okay?'

'Just got to work around the potholes, Sarge. Almost done. Hey, you know what I'm having? I'm having a brainstorm.'

'Stop. You'll hurt yourself.'

'No, listen to this. You know those people on the infomercials who make all that money with the stupid shit they sell? We could sell these damned suits to fat people, see? You just wear it and you lose weight.'

'Keep your damned head with that bomb, Riggio. How's your body temp?'

'I'm okay.'

In truth, he was so hot that he felt dizzy, but he wanted to make sure he had good clean shots. He circled the box like a man in a space suit, getting front, side, and off angles, then pointed the Real Time straight down for a top view. That's when he saw a shadow that hadn't been visible in the side views.

'Buck, you see that? I think I got something.'

'What?'

'Here in the overhead view. Take a snap.'

A thin, hairlike shadow emerged from the side of one pipe and extended up through the spool. This wire wasn't attached to the others, which confused Riggio until a sudden, unexpected thought occurred to him: Maybe the spool was there only to hide this other wire.

In that moment, fear crackled through him and his bowels clenched. He called out to Buck Daggett, but the words did not form.

Riggio thought, *Oh, God*.

The bomb detonated at a rate of twenty-eight thousand feet per second, twenty-two times faster than a nine-millimeter bullet leaves the muzzle of a pistol. Heat flashed outward in a burst of white light hot enough to melt iron. The air pressure spiked from a normal fifteen pounds per square inch to twenty-two hundred pounds, shattering the iron pipes into jagged shrapnel that punched through the Kevlar suit like hyperfast bullets. The shock wave slammed into his body with an overpressure of three hundred thousand pounds, crushing his chest, rupturing his liver, spleen, and lungs, and separating his unprotected hands. Charlie Riggio was lifted fourteen feet into the air and thrown a distance of thirty-eight feet.

Even this close to the point of detonation, Riggio might have survived if this had been, as he first suspected, a garage bomb cooked up by a gangbanger with makeshift materials.

It wasn't.

Bits of tarmac and steel fell around him like bloody rain, long after Charlie Riggio was dead.

Part One

CHAPTER ONE

'Tell me about the thumb. I know what you told me on the phone, but tell me everything now.'

Starkey inhaled half an inch of cigarette, then flicked ash on the floor, not bothering with the ashtray. She did that every time she was annoyed with being here, which was always.

'Please use the ashtray, Carol.'

'I missed.'

'You didn't miss.'

Detective-2 Carol Starkey took another deep pull on the cigarette, then crushed it out. When she first started seeing this therapist, Dana Williams wouldn't let her smoke during session. That was three years and four therapists ago. In the time Starkey was working her way through the second and third therapists, Dana had gone back to the smokes herself, and now didn't mind. Sometimes they both smoked and the goddamned room clouded up like the Imperial Valley capped by an inversion layer.

Starkey shrugged.

'No, I guess I didn't miss. I'm just pissed off, is all. It's been three years, and here I am back where I started.'

'With me.'

'Yeah. Like in three years I shouldn't be over this shit.'

'So tell me what happened, Carol. Tell me about the little girl's thumb.'

Starkey fired up another cigarette, then settled back to recall the little girl's thumb. Starkey was down to three packs a day. The progress should have made her feel better, but didn't.

'It was Fourth of July. This idiot down in Venice decides to make his own fireworks and give them away to the neighbors. A little girl ends up losing the thumb and index finger on her right hand, so we get the call from the emergency room.'

'Who is "we"?'

'Me and my partner that day, Beth Marzik.'

'Another woman?'

'Yeah. There's two of us in CCS.'

'Okay.'

'By the time we get down there, the family's gone home, so we go to the house. The father's crying, saying how they found the finger, but not the thumb, and then he shows us these homemade firecrackers that are so damned big she's lucky she didn't lose the hand.'

'He made them?'

'No, a guy in the neighborhood made them, but the father won't tell us. He says the man didn't mean any harm. I say, your daughter has been *maimed*, sir, other children are at *risk*, sir, but the guy won't cop. I ask the mother, but the guy says something in Spanish, and now she won't talk, either.'

'Why won't they tell you?'

'People are assholes.'

The world according to Carol Starkey, Detective-2 with LAPD's Criminal Conspiracy Section. Dana made a note of that in a leatherbound notebook, an act which Starkey never liked. The notes gave physical substance to her words, leaving Starkey feeling vulnerable because she thought of the notes as evidence.

Starkey had more of the cigarette, then shrugged and went on with it.

'These bombs are six inches long, right? We call'm Mexican Dynamite. So many of these things are going off, it sounds like the Academy pistol range, so Marzik and I start a door-to-door. But the neighbors are just like the father – no one's telling us anything, and I'm getting madder and madder. Marzik and I are walking back to the

12

car when I look down and there's the thumb. I just looked down and there it was, this beautiful little thumb, so I scooped it up and brought it back to the family.'

'On the phone, you told me you tried to make the father eat it.'

'I grabbed his collar and pushed it into his mouth. I did that.'

Dana shifted in her chair, Starkey reading from her body language that she was uncomfortable with the image. Starkey couldn't blame her.

'It's easy to understand why the family filed a complaint.'

Starkey finished the cigarette and crushed it out.

'The family didn't complain.'

'Then why— ?'

'Marzik. I guess I scared Marzik. She had a talk with my lieutenant, and Kelso threatened to send me to the bank for an evaluation.'

LAPD maintained its Behavorial Sciences Unit in the Far East Bank building on Broadway, in Chinatown. Most officers lived in abject fear of being ordered to the bank, correctly believing that it called into question their stability and ended any hope of career advancement. They had an expression for it: 'Overdrawn on the career account.'

'If I go to the bank, they'll never let me back on the Bomb Squad.'

'And you keep asking to go back?'

'It's all I've wanted since I got out of the hospital.'

Irritated now, Starkey stood and lit another cigarette. Dana studied her, which Starkey also didn't like. It made her feel watched, as if Dana was waiting for her to do or say something more that she could write down. It was a valid interview technique that Starkey used herself. If you said nothing, people felt compelled to fill the silence.

'The job is all I have left, damnit.'

Starkey regretted the defensive edge in her voice and

felt even more embarrassed when Dana again scribbled a note.

'So you told Lieutenant Kelso that you would seek help on your own?'

'Jesus, no. I kissed his ass to get out of it. I know I have a problem, Dana, but I'll get help in a way that doesn't fuck my career.'

'Because of the thumb?'

Starkey stared at Dana Williams with the same flat eyes she would use on Internal Affairs.

'Because I'm falling apart.'

Dana sighed, and a warmth came to her eyes that infuriated Starkey because she resented having to reveal herself in ways that made her feel vulnerable and weak. Carol Starkey did not do 'weak' well, and never had.

'Carol, if you came back because you want me to fix you as if you were broken, I can't do that. Therapy isn't the same as setting a bone. It takes time.'

'It's been three years. I should be over this by now.'

'There's no "should" here, Carol. Consider what happened to you. Consider what you survived.'

'I've had enough with *considering* it. I've *considered* it for three fucking years.'

A sharp pain began behind her eyes. Just from *considering* it.

'Why do you think you keep changing therapists, Carol?'

Starkey shook her head, then lied.

'I don't know.'

'Are you still drinking?'

'I haven't had a drink in over a year.'

'How's your sleep?'

'A couple of hours, then I'm wide awake.'

'Is it the dream?'

Carol felt herself go cold.

'No.'

'Anxiety attacks?'

Starkey was wondering how to answer when the pager

14

clipped to her waist vibrated. She recognized the number as Kelso's cell phone, followed by 911, the code the detectives in the Criminal Conspiracy Section used when they wanted an immediate response.

'Shit, Dana. I've gotta get this.'

'Would you like me to leave?'

'No. No, I'll just step out.'

Starkey took her purse out into the waiting room, where a middle-aged woman seated on the couch briefly met her eyes, then averted her face.

'Sorry.'

The woman nodded without looking.

Starkey dug through her purse for her cell phone, then punched the speed dial to return Kelso's page. She could tell he was in his car when he answered.

'It's me, Lieutenant. What's up?'

'Where are you?'

Starkey stared at the woman.

'I was looking for shoes.'

'I didn't ask what you were doing, Starkey. I asked where you were.'

She felt the flush of anger when he said it, and shame that she even gave a damn what he thought.

'The west side.'

'All right. The bomb squad had a call-out, and, um, I'm on my way there now. Carol, we lost Charlie Riggio. He was killed at the scene.'

Starkey's fingers went cold. Her scalp tingled. It was called 'going core'. The body's way of protecting itself by drawing the blood inward to minimize bleeding. A response left over from our animal pasts when the threat would involve talons and fangs and something that wanted to rip you apart. In Starkey's world, the threat often still did.

'Starkey?'

She turned away and lowered her voice so that the woman couldn't hear.

'Sorry, Lieutenant. Was it a bomb? Was it a device that went off?'

'I don't know the details yet, but, yes, there was an explosion.'

Sweat leaked from her skin, and her stomach clenched. Uncontrolled explosions were rare. A Bomb Squad officer dying on the job was even more rare. The last time it had happened was three years ago.

'Anyway, I'm on my way there now. Ah, Starkey, I could put someone else on this, if you'd rather I did that.'

'I'm up in the rotation, Lieutenant. It's my case.'

'All right. I wanted to offer.'

He gave her the location, then broke the connection. The woman on the couch was watching her as if she could read Starkey's pain. Starkey saw herself in the waiting-room mirror, abruptly white beneath her tan. She felt herself breathing. Shallow, fast breaths.

Starkey put her phone away, then went back to tell Dana that she would have to end their session early.

'We've got a call-out, so I have to go. Ah, listen, I don't want you to turn in any of this to the insurance, okay? I'll pay out of my own pocket, like before.'

'No one can get access to your insurance records, Carol. Not without your permission. You truly don't need to spend the money.'

'I'd rather pay.'

As Starkey wrote the check, Dana said, 'You didn't finish the story. Did you catch the man who made the firecrackers?'

'The little girl's mother took us to a garage two blocks away where we found him with eight hundred pounds of smokeless gunpowder. Eight hundred pounds, and the whole place is reeking of gasoline because you know what this guy does for a living? He's a gardener. If that place had gone up, it would've taken out the whole goddamned block.'

'My Lord.'

Starkey handed over the check, then said her good-byes

and started for the door. She stopped with her hand on the knob because she remembered something that she had intended to ask Dana.

'There's something about that guy I've been wondering about. Maybe you can shed some light.'

'In what way?'

'This guy we arrested, he tells us he's been building fireworks his whole life. You know how we know it's true? He's only got three fingers on his left hand and two on his right. He's blown them off one by one.'

Dana paled.

'I've arrested a dozen guys like that. We call them chronics. Why do they do that, Dana? What do you say about people like that who keep going back to the bombs?'

Now Dana took out a cigarette of her own and struck it. She blew out a fog of smoke and stared at Starkey before answering.

'I think they want to destroy themselves.'

Starkey nodded.

'I'll call you to reschedule, Dana. Thanks.'

Starkey went out to her car, keeping her head down as she passed the woman in the waiting room. She slid behind the wheel, but didn't start the engine. Instead, she opened her briefcase and took out a slim silver flask of gin. She took a long drink, then opened the door and threw up in the parking lot.

When she finished heaving, she put away the gin and ate a Tagamet.

Then, doing her best to get a grip on herself, Carol Starkey drove across town to a place exactly like the one where she had died.

Helicopters marked ground zero the way vultures circle roadkill, orbiting over the crime scene in layers like a cake. Starkey saw them just as the traffic locked down, half a mile from the incident site. She used her bubble flasher to edge into an Amaco station, left her car, and walked the remaining eight blocks.

A dozen radio units were on the scene, along with two Bomb Squad Suburbans and a growing army of media people. Kelso was standing near the forward Suburban with the Bomb Squad commander, Dick Leyton, and three of the day-shift bomb techs. Kelso was a short man with a droopy mustache, in a black-checked sport coat. Kelso noticed Starkey, and waved to catch her eye, but Starkey pretended she didn't see him.

Riggio's body lay in a heap in the parking lot, midway between the forward Suburban and the building. A coroner investigator was leaning against his van, watching an LAPD criminalist named John Chen work the body. Starkey didn't know the CI because she had never before worked a case where someone had died, but she knew Chen.

Starkey badged her way past the uniforms at the mouth of the parking lot. One of the uniforms, a younger guy she didn't know, said, 'Man, that dude got the shit blown out of himself. I wouldn't go over there, I was you.'

'You wouldn't?'

'Not if I had a choice.'

Smoking at a crime scene was against LAPD policy, but Starkey fired up before crossing the parking lot to confront Charlie Riggio's body. Starkey had known him from her days on the squad, so she expected this to be hard. It was.

Riggio's helmet and chest protector had been stripped off by the paramedics who had worked to revive him. Shrapnel had cut through the suit, leaving bloody puckers across his chest and stomach that looked blue in the bright afternoon sun. A single hole had been punched in his face, just beneath the left eye. Starkey glanced over at the helmet and saw that the Lexan faceplate was shattered. They said that the Lexan could stop a bullet from a deer rifle. Then she looked back at his body and saw that his hands were missing.

Starkey ate a Tagamet, then turned away so that she wouldn't have to see the body.

'Hey, John. What do we have here?'

'Hey, Starkey. You got the lead on this one?'

'Yeah. Kelso said that Buck Daggett was out, but I don't see him.'

'They sent him to the hospital. He's okay, but he's pretty shook. Leyton wanted him checked.'

'Okay. So what did he say? You got anything I can use?'

Chen glanced back at the body, then pointed out the Dumpster.

'The device was over by that Dumpster. Buck says Riggio was over it with the Real Time when it went off.'

Starkey followed his nod to a large piece of the Real Time portable X-ray that had been blown out into the street. She considered the Dumpster again, and guessed that the Real Time had been kicked more than forty yards. Riggio himself lay almost thirty yards from the Dumpster.

'Did Daggett or the medics pull him over here?'

Anytime there was an explosion, bomb techs were trained to expect a secondary device. She figured that Daggett would have pulled Riggio away from the Dumpster for that reason.

'You'd have to ask Daggett. I think this is where he fell.'

'Jesus. We gotta be, what, thirty yards from the detonation point?'

'Buck said it was a helluva blast.'

She guesstimated the distance again, then toed the body armor to examine the blast pattern. The suit looked as if twenty shotguns had been fired into it point-blank. She'd seen similar suit damage when 'dirty' bombs had gone off with a lot of fire and shrapnel, but this bomb had pushed the shrap through twelve layers of armor and had thrown a man thirty yards. The energy released must have been enormous.

Chen took a plastic bag from his evidence kit, pulling

the plastic tight to show her a piece of blackened metal about the size of a postage stamp.

'This is kind of interesting, too. It's a piece of the pipe frag I found stuck in his suit.'

Starkey looked close. A squiggly line had been etched into the metal.

'What is that, an *S*?'

Chen shrugged.

'Or some kind of symbol. Remember that bomb they found in San Diego last year, the one with dicks drawn all over it?'

Starkey ignored him. Chen liked to talk. If he got going about a bomb with dicks on it, she would never get her work done.

'John, do me a favor and swab some of the samples tonight, okay?'

Chen went sulky.

'It's going to be really late when I finish here, Carol. I've got to work the Dumpster, and then there's going to be whatever you guys find in the sweep. It's going to take me two or three hours just to log everything.'

They would search for pieces of the device everywhere within a hundred-yard radius, combing nearby rooftops, the faces of the apartment buildings and houses across the street, cars, the Dumpster, and the wall behind the Dumpster. They would search for anything and everything that might help them reconstruct the bomb or give them a clue to its origins.

'Don't whine, John. It's not cool.'

'I'm just saying.'

'How long does it take to cook through the gas chrom?'

The sulk became sullen and put-upon.

'Six hours.'

Residue from the explosive would be present on any fragments of the bomb they found, as well as in the blast crater and on Riggio's suit. Chen would identify the substance by cooking it through a gas chromatograph, a process which took six hours. Starkey knew how long it would take when she asked, but asked anyway to make Chen feel guilty about it taking so long.

'Couldn't you swab a couple of samples first, just to start a chrom, then log everything after? An explosive with this kind of energy potential could really narrow down the field of guys I'm looking at, John. You could give me a head start here.'

Chen hated to do anything that wasn't methodical and by the book, but he couldn't deny her point. He checked his watch, counting out the time.

'Let me see what time we finish here, okay? I'll try, but I can't guarantee anything.'

'I gave up on guarantees a long time ago.'

Buck Daggett's Suburban sat forty-eight paces from Riggio's body. Starkey counted as she walked.

Kelso and Leyton saw her coming and moved away from the others to meet her. Kelso's face was grim; Leyton's tense and professional. Leyton had been off shift when he'd gotten the call and had rushed over in jeans and a polo shirt.

Leyton smiled softly when their eyes met, and Starkey thought there was a sad quality to it. Leyton, the twelve-year commander of the Bomb Squad, had selected Carol Starkey for the squad, just as he'd selected Charlie Riggio and every other tech below the rank of sergeant-supervisor. He had sent her to the FBI's Bomb School in Alabama and had been her boss for three years. When she had been in the hospital, he had come every day after his shift to visit her, fifty-four consecutive days, and when she had fought to stay on the job, he had lobbied on her behalf. There wasn't anyone on the job she respected as much, or cared for as much.

Starkey said, 'Dick, I want to walk the scene as soon as possible. Could we use as many of your people as you can get out?'

'Everyone not on duty is coming out. You've got us all.'

She turned to Kelso.

'Lieutenant, I'd like to talk to these Rampart guys to see if we can't conscript some of their uniforms to help.'

Kelso was frowning at her.

'I've already arranged it with their supervisor. You shouldn't be smoking here, Starkey.'

'Sorry. I'd better go talk to him, then, and get things organized.'

She made no move to put out her cigarette, and Kelso ignored the obvious rebellion.

'Before you do, you'll be working with Marzik and Santos on this.'

Starkey felt another Tagamet craving.

'Does it have to be Marzik?'

'Yes, Starkey, it has to be Marzik. They're inbound now. And something else. Lieutenant Leyton says we might have a break here before we get started: 911 got a call on this.'

She glanced at Leyton.

'Do we have a wit?'

'An Adam car took the call, but Buck told me they were responding to Emergency Services. If that's the case, then we should have a tape and an address.'

That was a major break.

'Okay. I'll get on it. Thanks.'

Kelso glanced toward the press again, frowning when he saw an LAPD media officer approaching them.

'I think we'd better go make a statement, Dick.'

'Be right there.'

Kelso scurried over to intercept the media officer while Leyton stayed with Starkey. They waited until the other man was gone, then Leyton considered her.

'How you doing, Carol?'

'I'm fine, Lieutenant. Kicking ass and taking names, like always. I'd still like to come back to the squad.'

Leyton found it within himself to nod. They had weathered that pounding three years ago, and both of them knew that the LAPD Personnel Unit would never allow it.